DATE DUE

JUN 8 1987

MAI NOV 1 3 1989

POOR STAINLESS

POOR STAINLESS

A New Story about the Borrowers

MARY NORTON

Illustrated by Beth and Joe Krush

Harcourt Brace Jovanovich, Inc.
New York

FIRST EDITION

A B C D E F G H I J

Hardbound edition ISBN 0-15-263221-2
Library edition ISBN 0-15-263222-0
Library of Congress Catalog Card Number: 70-140781

PRINTED IN THE UNITED STATES OF AMERICA

To *Lionel*

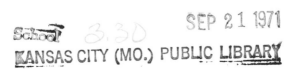

Where, we
sometimes ask ourselves, do all
the sewing needles go? And the drawing
pins, the matchboxes, the hairpins, the thimbles,
the safety pins? Factories go on making safety pins,
and people go on buying safety pins, and yet there
never is a safety pin just when you want one. Where are
they all? Now, at this minute? They cannot all just be
lying somewhere about the house. Who takes them and
why? It must—one begins to realize—be something or
someone who is living quite close beside us, under the same
roof; something or someone with human tastes and almost
human needs; something (or someone) very secret, very hidden
—under the floorboards, maybe, or behind the wall paneling.
Very small, of course—that stands to reason—and very busy, always improvising, always "making do." And brave—they must
be very brave to venture out into the vast human rooms (as
dangerous to them as such rooms are to mice) seeking the
wherewithal on which to sustain their lives. Who could
grudge them the odd pencil stub, the occasional bottle
top, the used postage stamp, or the leftover sliver
of cheese? No (it takes all kinds, as they say,
to make a world): we should accept their hidden presence and gently leave them
alone. Children call them "The
Borrowers."

"AND NOW," said Arrietty to Homily, "tell me what-you-used-to-do. . . ."

The phrase, run together in one eager breath, had lost its meaning as words. It described an activity, a way of passing the time while engaged in monotonous tasks. They were unpicking sequins from a square of yellowed chiffon: Homily unpicked while Arrietty threaded the glimmering circles on a string of pale blue silk. It was a fine spring day, and they sat beside the grating let into the outside wall. The sunlight fell across them in crisscross squares, and the soft air moved their hair.

9

"Well," said Homily, after a moment, "did I ever tell you about the time when I lit the big candle?"

"And burned a hole in the floorboards—and in the carpet upstairs? And human beans shrieked—and your father beat you with a wax matchstick? Yes, you've told me."

"It was a candle my father borrowed to melt down for dips. It shined lovely," said Homily.

"Tell me about the time when the cook upstairs upset the boiling marmalade and it all leaked down between the cracks—"

"Oh, that was dreadful," said Homily, "but we bottled it, or most of it, in acorn cups and an empty tube called morphia. But the mess, oh dear, the mess—my mother was beside herself. There was a corner of our carpet," added Homily reflectively, "which tasted sweet for months." With a work-worn hand she smoothed down the gleaming chiffon, which billowed smokelike on the moving air.

"I know what," cried Arrietty suddenly. "Tell me about the rat!"

"Oh, not again," said Homily.

She glanced at herself in a sequin which—to her—was about the size of a hand mirror. "I'm going very gray," she said. She polished up the sequin with a corner of her apron and stared again, patting her hair at the temples. "Did I ever tell you about Poor Stainless?"

"Who was he?" asked Arrietty.

"One of the Knife Machine boys."

"No . . ." said Arrietty, uncertainly.

"That was the first time I went upstairs. To look for Stainless." Homily, staring into the sequin, lifted her hair a little at the temples. "Oh dear," she said, in a slightly dispirited voice.

"I like it gray," said Arrietty warmly, gently retrieving the sequin, "it suits you. What about Poor Stainless—"

"He was lost, you see. And we were all to go up and look for him. It was an order," said Homily. "Some people thought it wrong that the women should go, too, but there it was: it was an order."

"Who gave it?" asked Arrietty.

"The grandfathers, of course. It was the first time I ever saw the scullery. After that, once I knew the way, I used to sneak up there now and again, but no one ever knew. Oh dear, I shouldn't say this to you!"

"Never mind," said Arrietty.

"Poor Stainless. He was the youngest of that family. They used to live down a hole in the plaster on a level with the table where the knife machine used to stand. They did all their borrowing in the scullery. Practically vegetarians they were—carrots, turnips, watercress, celery, peas, beans— the lot. All the stuff Crampfurl, the gardener, used to bring in in baskets. Lovely complexions they had, every one of them. Especially Stainless. Stainless had cheeks like apple-blossom. 'Merry little angel' my mother used to call him. All the grownups were mad about Stainless—he had a kind of way with them. But not with us. We didn't like him."

"Why not?" asked Arrietty, suddenly interested.

"I don't know," said Homily. "He had mean ways—well, more like teasing kind of ways; and he never got found out. He'd coax black beetles down our chute—great things with horns they were—and we'd know it was him, but we couldn't

prove it. And many a time he'd creep along above our floor-boards, with a bent pin on a string and hook at me through a crack in our ceiling: if we had a party, he'd do it, because he was too young to be asked. But it wasn't any fun, getting hooked by Stainless—caught me by the hair, once he did. And in those days," said Homily complacently, taking up another sequin, "my hair was my crowning glory." She stared into the sequin reflectively, then put it down with a sigh.

"Well, anyway," she went on briskly, "Stainless disappeared. What a to-do! His mother, it seemed, had sent him out to borrow parsley. Eleven-fifteen in the morning it was, and by evening he hadn't returned. And he didn't return that night.

"Now you must understand about parsley—it's a perfectly simple borrow and a quick one. Five minutes, it should have taken him: all you had to do was to walk along the knife machine table onto a ledge at the top of the wainscot, drop down (quite a small drop) onto the drainboard, and the parsley always stood in an old jam jar at the back of the sink—on a zinc shelf, like, with worn holes in it.

"Some said, afterwards, Stainless was too young to be sent for parsley. They blamed the parents. But there was his mother, single-handed behind the knife machine, getting a meal for all that family and the elder ones off borrowing with their father, and, as I told you, Stainless was always out anyway directly his mother's back was turned, plaguing us and what not and whispering down the cracks—'I see you,' he'd say. There was no privacy with Stainless until my father wall-papered our ceiling. Well, anyway," went on Homily, pausing to get her breath, "Stainless had disappeared, and the next day, a lovely sunny afternoon, at three o'clock sharp we were all to go up and look for him. It was Mrs. Driver the cook's afternoon out, and the maids would be having their rest.

"We all had our orders: some were to look among the garden boots and the blacking brushes; others in the vegetable bins; my father and your Uncle Hendreary's father and several of the stronger men had to carry a wrench with a wooden spoon lashed across it to unscrew the trap in the drain below the sink.

"I stopped to watch this, I remember. Several of us did. Round and round they went—like Crampfurl does with the cider press—on the bottom of an upturned bucket under the sink. Suddenly, there was a great clatter and the screw came tumbling off and there was a rush of greasy water all over the bucket top. Oh dear, oh dear," exclaimed Homily, laughing a little but half ashamed of doing so, "those poor men! None of their wives would have them home again until they had climbed up into the sink proper and had the tap turned on them. *Then* it was the hot tap, which was meant to be lukewarm. Oh dear, oh dear, what a to-do! But still no Stainless.

"We young ones were taken home then, but it was a good four hours before the men abandoned the search. We ate our tea in silence, I remember, while our mothers sniffed and wiped their eyes. After tea, my younger brother started playing marbles with three old dried peas he had, and my mother rebuked him and said, 'Quiet now—have you no respect? Think of your father and of all those brave men Upstairs!' The way she said 'Upstairs' made your hair stand on end.

"And yet, you know, Arrietty, I liked the scullery, what I'd seen of it—with the sunshine coming through the yard door and falling warm on that old brick floor. And the bunches of bay leaf and dried thyme. But I did remember there had been a mousetrap under the sink and another under the bottom shelf of the boot cupboard. Not that these were dangerous—except for those who did not know. Our father would roll a potato at them, and then they would go click. But they'd jump a bit when they did it, and that's what startled you. No, the real danger was Crampfurl, the gardener, coming in suddenly through the yard door with the vegetables for dinner; or Mrs. Driver, the cook, back from her afternoon out, to fill a kettle. And there were other maids then in the house who might take a fancy to a radish or an apple from the barrel behind the scullery door.

"Anyway, when darkness came, the rescue party was called off. Our mothers made a great fuss of the men, thankful to see them back, and brought them their suppers and fetched their slippers. And no one spoke above a whisper. And we were sent to bed.

"By that time, we, too, felt grave. As we lay cozily under

16

the warm covers, we could not help but think of Stainless. Poor Stainless. Perhaps he'd gone *past* the trap and down the drain of the sink into the sewers. We knew there were borrowers who lived in sewers and that they were dreadful people, wild and fierce like rats. Once, my little brother played with one and got bitten in the arm and his shirt stolen. And he got a dreadful rash.

"Next day, the two grandfathers called another meeting: they were the elders, like, and always made the decisions. One grandfather was my father's great-uncle. I forget now who the other was . . ."

"Never mind," said Arrietty.

"Well," said Homily, "the long and short of it was—we were all to go Upstairs and go throughout every room. That old house, Firbank, was full of borrowers in those days—or so it seemed—and some we never knew. But we was to seek them out, any we could find, and ask about Poor Stainless. A house-to-house search they called it."

"Goodness!" gasped Arrietty.

"We was all to go," said Homily.

"Women and children, too?"

"*All*," said Homily, "except the little 'uns."

She sat still, frowning into space. Her face seemed graven by the memory. "Some said the old men were mad," she went on, after a moment. "But it was wonderfully organized: we were to go in twos—two to each room. The elder ones and the young girls for the ground floor, the younger men and some quite young boys for the creepers."

"What creepers?"

17

"The creepers up the house front—the vines—of course: they had to search the bedrooms!"

"Yes, I see," said Arrietty.

"That was the only way you could get above the ground floor in those days. It was long before your father invented his hatpin with a bit of tape tied on. There was no way to tackle the stairs—the height of the treads, you see, and nothing to grip on . . ."

"Yes. Go on about the creepers."

"Early dawn it was, barely light, when the young lads were lined up on the gravel, marking from below which of the windows was open. One, two, three, GO—and they was off —all the ivy and wisteria leaves shaking like a palsy! Oh, the stories they had to tell about what they found in those bed-rooms, but never a sign of Stainless! One poor little lad slipped on a windowsill and gripped on a cord to save himself. It was the cord of a roller blind, and the roller blind went clattering up to the ceiling and there he was—hanging on a thing like a wooden acorn. He got down in the end—swung himself back and forth until he got a grip on the valance, then down the curtain by the bobbles. Not much fun, though, with two great human beings in nightcaps, snoring away on the bed.

"We girls and the women took the downstairs rooms, each with a man who knew the ropes, like. We had orders to be back by teatime, because of the little 'uns, but the men were to search on until dusk. I had my Uncle Bolty, and they'd given us the morning room. And it was on that spring day, just after it became light"—Homily paused significantly— "that I first saw the Overmantels!"

18

"Oh," exclaimed Arrietty, "I remember—those proud kind of borrowers who lived above the chimneypiece?"

"Yes," said Homily, "them." She thought for a moment. "You never could tell how many of them there were because you always saw them doubled in the looking glass. The overmantel went right up to the ceiling, filled with shelves and twisty pillars and plush-framed photographs. You saw them always gliding about behind the cape gooseberries or the jars of pipe cleaners or the Japanese fans. They smelled of cigars and brandy and—something else. But perhaps that was the smell of the room. Russian leather—yes, that was it . . ."

"Go on," said Arrietty. "Did they speak to you?"

"Speak to us! Did the Overmantels speak to us!" Homily gave a short laugh, then shook her head grimly as though dismissing a memory. Her cheeks had become very pink.

"But," said Arrietty, breaking the odd silence, "at least you saw them!"

"Oh, we saw them right enough. And heard them. There were plenty of them about that morning. It was early, you see, and they knew the human beings were asleep. There they all were, gliding about, talking and laughing among themselves—and dressed up to kill for a mouse hunt. And they saw us all right, as we stood beside the door, but would they look at us? No, not they. Not straight, that is: their eyes slid about all the time as they laughed and talked among themselves. They looked past us and over us and under us, but never quite at us. Long, long eyes they had, and funny, light tinkling voices. You couldn't make out what they said.

"After a while, my Uncle Bolty stepped forward: he

cleared his throat and put on his very best voice (he could do this, you see—that's why they chose him for the morning room). 'Excuse and pardon me,' he said (it was lovely the way he said it), 'for troubling and disturbing you, but have you by any chance seen—' and he went on to describe Poor Stainless, lovely complexion and all.

"Not a sign of notice did he get. Those Overmantels just went on laughing and talking and putting on airs like as if they were acting on a stage. And beautiful they looked, too (you couldn't deny it), some of the women in their long-necked Overmantel way. The early morning sunlight shining on all that looking glass lit them all up, like, to a kind of pinky gold. Lovely it was. You couldn't help but notice . . .

"My Uncle Bolty began to look angry, and his face grew very red. 'High or low, we're borrowers all,' he said in a loud voice, 'and this little lad'—he almost shouted it—'was the apple of his mother's eye!' But the Overmantels went on talking in a silly, flustered way, laughing a little still and sliding their long eyes sideways.

"My Uncle Bolty suddenly lost his temper, 'All right,' he thundered, forgetting his special voice and going back to his country one, 'you silly, feckless lot. High you may be, but remember this—them as dwells below the kitchen floor has solid earth to build on, and we'll outlast you yet!'

"With that he turns away, and I go after him crying a little—I wouldn't know for why. Knee-high we were in the pile of the morning room carpet. As we passed through the doorway, a silence fell behind us. We waited in the hall and listened for a while. It was a long, long silence."

Arrietty did not speak. She sat there lost in thought and

gazing at her mother. After a moment, Homily sighed and said, "Somehow, I don't seem to forget that morning, though nothing much happened really—when you come to think of it. Some of the others had terrible adventures, especially them who was sent to search the bedrooms. But your Great Uncle Bolty was right. When they closed up most of the house, after her ladyship's hunting accident, the morning room wasn't used anymore. Starved out, they must have been, those Overmantels. Or frozen out." She sighed again and shook her head. "You can't help but feel sorry for them . . .

"We all stayed up that night, even us young ones, waiting and hoping for news. The search parties kept arriving back in ones and twos. There was hot soup for all, and some were given brandy. Some of the mothers looked quite gray with worry, but they kept up a good front, caring for all and sundry as they came tumbling in down the chute. By morning, all the searchers were home. The last to arrive were three young lads who had gotten trapped in the bedrooms when the housemaids came up at dusk to close the windows and draw the curtains. It had come on to rain, you see. They had to crouch inside the fender for over an hour while two great human beings changed for dinner. It was a lady and gentleman, and as they dressed, they quarreled—and it was all to do with someone called 'Algy.' Algy this and Algy that . . . on and on. Scorched and perspiring as these poor boys were, they peered out through the brass curlicues of the fender and took careful note of everything. At one point, the lady took off most of her hair and hung it on a chair back. The boys were astonished. At another point, the gentleman—taking off his socks— flung them across the room, and one landed in the fireplace. The boys were terrified and pulled it out of sight; it was a woolen sock and might begin to singe; they couldn't risk the smell."

24

"How did they get away?"

"Oh, that was easy enough once the room was empty and the guests were safely at dinner. They unraveled the sock, which had a hole in the toe, and let themselves down through the banisters on the landing. The first two got down all right. But the last, the littlest one, was hanging in air when the butler came up with a soufflé. All was well, though—the butler didn't look up, and the little one didn't let go.

"Well, that was that. The search was called off, and for us younger ones at least, life seemed to return to normal. Then one afternoon—it must have been a week later because it was a Saturday, I remember, and that was the day our mother always took a walk down the drainpipe to have tea with the Rain Barrels, and on this particular Saturday she took our little brother with her. Yes, that was it. Anyway, we two girls, my sister and I, found ourselves alone in the house. Our mother always left us jobs to do, and that afternoon it was to cut up a length of black shoelace to make armbands in memory of Stainless. Everybody was making them—it was an order 'to show respect'—and we were all to put them on together in three days' time. After a while, we forgot to be sad and chattered and laughed as we sewed. It was so peaceful, you see, sitting there together and with no fear any more of black beetles.

"Suddenly my sister looked up, as though she had heard a noise. 'What's that?' she said, and she looked kind of frightened.

"We both of us looked round the room. Then I heard her let out a cry: she was staring at a knothole in the ceiling.

Then I saw it, too—something moving in the knothole. It seemed to be black, but it wasn't a beetle. We could neither of us speak or move: we just sat there riveted—watching this thing come winding down toward us out of the ceiling. It was a shiny snaky sort of thing, and it had a twist or curl in it which, as it got lower, swung round in a blind kind of way and drove us shrieking into a corner. We clung together, crying and staring, until suddenly my sister said, 'Hush!' We waited, listening. 'Someone spoke,' she whispered, staring toward the ceiling. Then we heard it—a hoarse voice, rather breathy and horribly familiar. 'I can see you!' it said.

"We were furious. We called him all sorts of names. We threatened him with every kind of punishment. We implored him to take the Thing away. But all he did was to giggle a little and keep on saying, in that silly singsong voice: "Taste it . . . taste it . . . it's lovely!"

"Oh," breathed Arrietty, "did you dare?"

Homily frowned. "Yes. In the end. And it was lovely," she admitted grudgingly. "It was a licorice bootlace."

"But where had he been all that time?"

"In the village shop."

"But—" Arrietty looked incredulous. "How did he get there?"

"It was all quite simple really. Mrs. Driver had left her shopping basket on the scullery table, with a pair of shoes to be heeled. Stainless, on his way to the parsley, heard her coming and nipped inside a shoe. Mrs. Driver put the shoes in the basket and carried them off to the village. She put down the basket on the shop counter while she gossiped a while

with the postmistress, and seizing the right opportunity, Stainless scrambled out."

"But how did he get back home again?"

"The next time Mrs. Driver went in for the groceries, of course. He was in a box of haircombs at the time, but he recognized the basket."

Arrietty looked thoughtful. "Poor Stainless," she said,

after a moment, "what an experience! He must have been terrified."

"Terrified! Stainless! Not he! He'd enjoyed every minute of it!" Homily's voice rose. "He'd had one wild, wicked, wonderful, never-to-be-forgotten week of absolute, glorious freedom—living on jujubes, walnut whips, chocolate bars, bulls'-eyes, hundreds and thousands, and still lemonade. And what had he done to deserve it?" The chiffon between Homily's fingers seemed to dance with indignation. "That's what we asked ourselves! We didn't like it. Not after all we'd been through: we never did think it was fair!" Crossly, she shook out the chiffon and, with lips set, began to fold it. But gradually, as she smoothed her hands across the frail silk, her movements became more gentle: she looked thoughtful suddenly, and as Arrietty watched, a little smile began to form at the corners of her mouth. "There was one thing, though, that we all took note of . . ." she said slowly, after a moment.

"What was that?" asked Arrietty.

"His cheeks had gone all pasty-like, and his eyes looked" —she hesitated, seeking the word—"sort of *piggy*. There was a big red spot on his nose and a pink one on his chin. Yes," she went on, thinking this over, "all that sugar, you see! Poor Stainless! Pity, really, when you come to think of it"—she smiled again and slightly shook her head—"good times or no good times, to have lost that wonderful complexion."